TIMMY
and the Otters

by
Jeremy Moray

Illustrated by
Dee Gale

Harbour Publishing

AUTHOR'S NOTE

Again my thanks are due to those people whose generosity and infinite patience have made possible yet another Timmy book!

Particularly I would like to thank Stephanie Hewlett of the Vancouver Public Aquarium, Lens and Shutter and, of course, my mentor in these tugging matters, Gary Kleaman of Lionsgate Tug and Barge Ltd.

J.M.

Canadian Cataloguing in Publication Data

Moray, Jeremy, 1943–
Timmy and the otters

ISBN 1-55017-007-4
I. Gale, D.   II. Title
PS8576. O73T52   jC813'.54   C81-091353-4
PZ7.M673Timm   1981

Published by
Harbour Publishing Co. Ltd.
P.O. Box 219
Madeira Park, BC Canada V0N 2H0

Printed and bound in Hong Kong by Colorcraft

First edition	1981
Reprinted	1985
Reprinted	1987
Reprinted	1989

for
Oliver

ANOTHER AUTHOR'S NOTE

Don't forget to follow the story on the chart at
the back of this book.

J.M.

Early one summer morning, Timmy the Tug left his mooring in False Creek. He was going to Woodfibre Mill near Squamish to collect a barge and take it to Victoria. Captain Jones and Frank were in the wheelhouse drinking their morning mugs of tea. Matilda the cat was curled up on the chart table trying to sleep. It was far too early for her.

As they approached Point Atkinson, Timmy was looking out for his friend Simon the seagull. Simon had been to his cousin's birthday party the day before, and had stayed overnight. He had said he would meet them by the lighthouse.

By the time Timmy was passing the end of Bowen Island, he was very worried. 'Simon is never late for a trip,' he thought. 'I know he wanted to go on to Victoria with us, later to-day.'

Suddenly, a gull flew round Timmy, squawking loudly. Captain Jones slowed Timmy down and the gull landed on his foredeck.

"I'm one of Simon's cousins. My name is Sylvia," she said.

"Where's Simon?" asked Timmy. "Is he alright?"

"Well, yes. But there's been a terrible accident and we need your help," continued Sylvia.

Matilda joined them on the foredeck.

"Tell us what's happened to poor Simon," Timmy pleaded.

Sylvia told them about the birthday party on Hermit Island and the feast. When she was describing all the seafood goodies, Matilda couldn't help licking her lips, and looking hungrily at Sylvia.

"After the feast," Sylvia continued. "We had a swimming race out to a deadhead. Simon was halfway, when a big oil slick washed all around him and the other gulls. Luckily for some of us, we had felt too full to play, and had stayed on the beach."

"Oh, no!" cried Timmy. "Poor Simon; how can we help him and your friends?"

"There's an old man who lives on the island. He is trying to clean the oil off their feathers. He needs lots of fish to feed them until they can fly again."

Captain Jones had been leaning out of the wheelhouse window listening. "That slick must have come from one of those big ships," he said. "They should take more care."

Timmy was very unhappy. Two large tears rolled down the front of the wheelhouse and splashed onto the deck.

"Don't worry, Timmy," Captain Jones continued. "I'm sure we can help."

"Why don't we get Sally the Seal to catch some fish for us?" suggested Frank.

"Good idea," said Captain Jones. "Sylvia; you fly ahead to Anvil Island. Ask Sally to round up her friends and meet us on the other side of Bowen Island. We'll drop the little boat into the water and they can fill it with fish. Then Timmy can tow it to Hermit Island."

As Sylvia flew away, Captain Jones put Timmy's engine at full speed ahead. Timmy felt much happier now he knew he could help the seagulls.

Matilda climbed back into the wheelhouse. She sat looking out of the window. All this talk of seafood feasts, and now boat loads of fish made her feel very hungry. 'Those birds and all that fish. What about me?' she thought sulkily.

Captain Jones began to stroke her, as he saw her tail twitching, crossly. "Not enough attention, eh, old cat?" he laughed.

Soon they entered Barfleur Passage and stopped by Keats Island. While they were waiting for Sally and her friends, Derek and John, the deckhands, winched the little yellow boat into the water.

Matilda was getting very excited at the thought of seeing all the fish. She stretched out on Timmy's rail waiting for the fun to begin. Suddenly, Sally surfaced right below her.

"Hello, Matilda," she called. "We've come to collect fish for Simon and his friends."

"That's great," said Matilda. "But Sally, why don't you throw one onto the deck for me?" Matilda purred in a loud whisper, hoping no one else would hear.

Sally grinned and gave several honks. Immediately Timmy was surrounded by seals.

"O.K., Sally," called Frank. "Fill 'er up!"

They all watched as seal after seal surfaced and threw a fish into the little yellow boat. Matilda had never seen so many fish before. As she leant further and further over the side, Derek put a hand on her.

"You silly cat. You'll fall off, if you lean out like that," he laughed.

Soon the boat was full of flapping fish. Captain Jones asked Sally to follow them, as they steamed slowly towards Hermit Island. "You'll have to push it through the shallow water to the beach," he called.

When they were close to the island, Timmy could see the old man waving from the beach. Also, he could see groups of seagulls huddled around a fire.

"Wonderful, wonderful," called the old man, as the seals pushed the boat into the beach. "Thank you very much. Your friend Simon should be better in a day or so," he called to Timmy as he unloaded the fish.

"Good luck, Simon," called Timmy and he smiled as he saw the old man give Simon a big fish.

"We must be going, if we're to be in Victoria tonight," said Captain Jones, climbing back into the wheelhouse. "We've still got to collect the barge from Woodfibre."

They all said goodbye to the seals and Sylvia, and thanked them for their help. With the small boat loaded on the roof again, they were soon steaming up Montague Channel. Matilda was in the galley watching Frank clean one of the salmon. She sat on the bench and watched every move.

"Alright, you greedy monster," Frank said. "You can have a piece from the tail."

Matilda grinned as Frank put a large piece of salmon in her bowl and placed it on the table for her.

Later that morning they were towing the empty barge down Georgia Strait to Victoria. They were going to collect a load of lumber, and bring it back to False Creek. The sea was calm, and the sun was shining. Timmy sang to himself as he chugged along, watching the other boats sailing in the straits.

In the early afternoon he approached the entrance to Active Pass. He heard Captain Jones calling on the radio to warn the other boats — "Timmy the Tug is coming through the pass with a barge." He smiled as people waved to him from a ferry turning into Sturdies Bay on Galiano Island.

Derek went back to the aft deck. Timmy felt his big green winch rumbling, as the tow line was being shortened. Now the barge was more under control in the narrow waters.

As Frank steered Timmy between the islands, Captain Jones went out on the side deck. He looked at the little houses dotted among the trees. 'It would be nice to live on one of the islands, when I retire next year,' he thought.

They steamed on between Moresby Island and Stuart Island, and turned right around Discovery Island. Half an hour later, the long seawall of Victoria harbour came into sight.

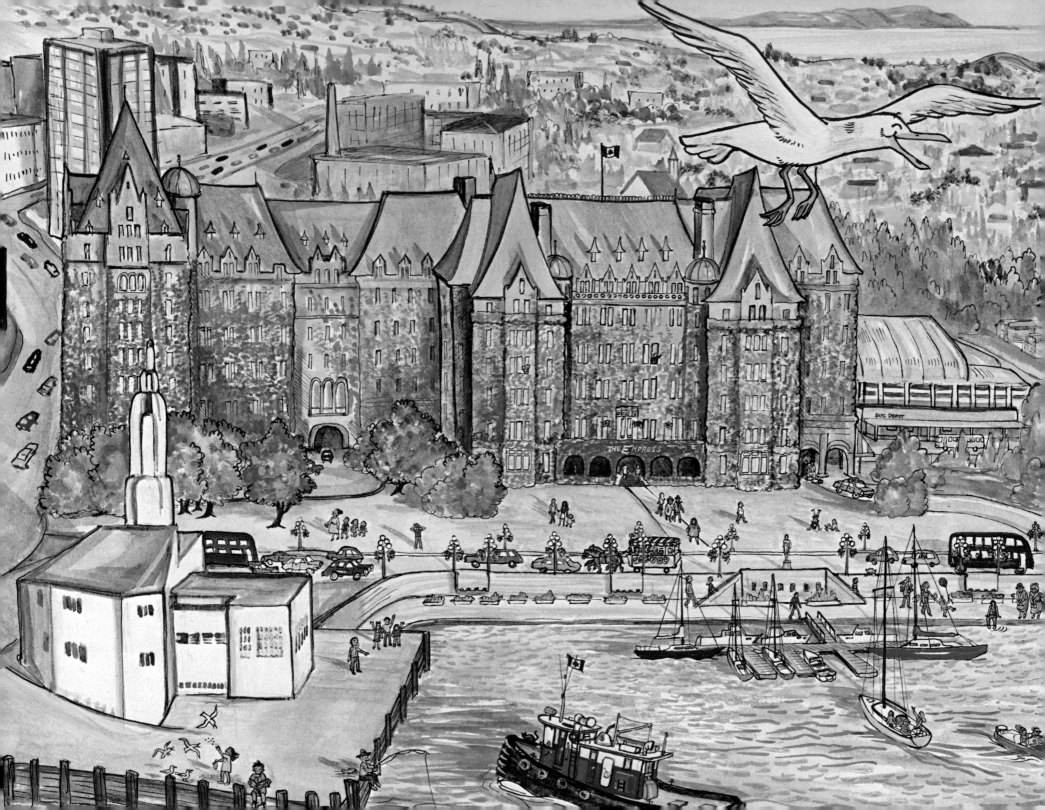

Soon Timmy was nudging the big red and white barge up against the wharf. There were huge piles of lumber high above him.

"We'll have this loaded for you by tomorrow morning," called one of the men who was tying up the barge.

"Thank you," replied Captain Jones. "We're going to spend the night in the inner harbour."

'Great!' thought Timmy. 'There's always lots going on in there.'

Captain Jones took Timmy very slowly into the inner harbour. As they approached the quayside, opposite the Parliament buildings, a group of people gathered to watch him being tied up.

Timmy felt very proud as he bobbed up and down on the little waves made by the yachts coming and going to the floats below the Empress Hotel.

"Time to get smartened up," Frank said, giving Matilda a pat. "We're going to spend the night with friends of Captain Jones."

Matilda wasn't very pleased at the idea. She knew she would have to spend the evening being lifted onto people's laps, and stroked endlessly. And even worse, she would be fed dried cat food. 'Ugh!' she thought. 'Give me fresh fish, or a tender bird, any day.'

As Derek and John tidied Timmy's ropes and washed down the decks, Captain Jones, Frank and Matilda set off for their friend's house.

Timmy was very happy watching the boats and seaplanes, and all the people walking along the harbour-side. As it began to get dark the Parliament buildings were lit up by strings of lights. They looked like a magic castle in a fairy tale. Soon a big orange moon climbed into the sky above the Empress Hotel. Timmy smiled, and went happily to sleep.

The next morning, while John cooked breakfast, Frank took Matilda shopping. They were walking up Government Street, when Matilda saw some pidgeons playing on the sidewalk.

She decided it would be fun to give them a fright, so she raced after them. They were too quick for her, and flew up onto a roof. "Great fat birds," she snorted as people laughed at her. "Didn't think they would be able to fly!"

"Come in here," called Frank as he reached the old tobacco shop. "We'll buy Captain Jones some of his favourite pipe tobacco."

Then they bought some brass polish for Timmy, all sorts of food for the journey home; and, as a special treat, a large, juicy rock cod for Matilda. She could hardly wait to get back on board.

Frank and Matilda climbed onto Timmy just as breakfast was being served. When they had finished, Captain Jones took Timmy back to the outer harbour. Soon he had his barge in tow, loaded with lumber.

As they passed the end of the seawall, Timmy turned eastwards towards Trial Island. Suddenly, he heard loud barking noises. He looked over towards the island.

"Hey! 'It's a whole group of sea lions," he shouted excitedly.

"So it is," said Captain Jones. "They must have come up from California. Normally, they go north in the spring, and stop off here to get married."

Matilda rushed out on deck followed by the rest of the crew, just as a large sea lion surfaced beside Timmy. As soon as she saw the big furry animal below her, she ran back into the wheelhouse, and stared bravely out of the window. "Imagine swimming all the way from California just to get married," she muttered to herself.

"You're late going north this year, aren't you?" called Frank.

"Yes; the water's been too cold up to now, so we decided to go north a bit later," barked the big sea lion. "And some of those young fellows are staying behind. We'll pick them up on our way back south in the fall."

Timmy wished them a safe journey, and gave them a loud 'toot'.

As Timmy approached Active Pass, he heard Captain Jones call again on the radio. Then he was steered very slowly and carefully through all the little fishing boats, crowding around Helen Point.

John had been working the winch to bring the barge up close to the stern. As he walked back along the side deck, he saw a long piece of thick rope floating in the water, right beside Timmy.

"Look out Cap'n," he yelled. "Rope!"

Before Captain Jones could steer Timmy clear, there was a terrible grinding noise from the engine room, and Timmy's propeller stopped.

"The prop's fouled," boomed Captain Jones. "Frank, get the anchor over quickly."

Frank jumped from the wheelhouse and called John to help him on the foredeck. Timmy started drifting backwards on the tide, towards the bank. John and Frank heaved the big anchor over the bow, and let out a long length of chain. Nearer and nearer to the bank they drifted.

"Clattering clams!" cried Timmy. "I hope the anchor holds, otherwise we'll be on the rocks! Now what are we going to do? I can't move without my propeller."

Matilda had climbed onto the rail to watch what was happening. "Don't worry, Timmy, we'll be alright," she purred, bravely. But she was just as frightened as Timmy.

Suddenly, there was a jerk. Matilda nearly fell into the water. Captain Jones leant out of the wheelhouse window.

"The anchor's holding," he called to the crew. "Now we must get the rope untangled as quickly as possible. There'll be a ferry coming through before long."

"I'll try and free it with the boathook," John said as he ran back to the aft deck. "If not, we'll have to go over the side. I hope the water's not too cold." He smiled at Derek who had come out of the galley to see if he could help.

"Look over there," Derek said. "There's a whole family of otters having a picnic. Maybe they would come and help us."

"I'll go and ask them," said Matilda, eyeing their picnic baskets. "I can jump onto that dead tree sticking out from the bank, and get ashore." She crouched on the rail, and sprang out over the water. She just managed to land on the end of the tree. She walked along it very carefully towards the bank.

"Well done, Matilda," called Timmy.

"She's certainly a brave cat," chuckled Frank.

Matilda scampered up the grassy bank to where the otter family were sitting around a blanket covered with plates of food. There was a pile of big red crabs, black shiny mussels, opened oysters, clam cookies, sea urchin sandwiches; and lying on a bed of bright green leaves was a glistening red snapper.

Grandpa otter was lying in the shade of a tree, reading a copy of the Seabed Times, his daily newspaper. He put down his paper as Matilda approached, and stared over the top of his glasses.

"What do you want, cat?" he asked.

Matilda stopped. He seemed very stern. "Hello," she said, a little afraid. "I've come from Timmy the Tug to ask for your help."

"Yes," replied grandpa otter. "I saw you getting into trouble." He smiled. "I'm sure we can help you. But we'd better get on with it, or the tide will drop and you'll be sitting on the bottom."

"Oh, thank you; let's go quickly!" said Matilda looking longingly over her shoulder at the sumptuous seafood spread.

They all ran down to the bank and Matilda walked back along the tree trunk, as the otters flopped into the water.

"Here you are, Captain Jones," she called. "They've come to help."

"Good," replied Captain Jones. "We've got a rope tangled round Timmy's propeller and we need to cut it free," he called to grandpa otter.

"That's no problem," he said. "Give us a knife and I'll send a couple of pups down and we'll see what we can do."

So, as Grandpa otter lay on his back on the surface supervising the operation, the pups got to work underwater.

Matilda did not jump back onto Timmy. She had other ideas. Once the otters were busy, she sneaked back along the tree onto the bank. She raced across the grass, and stopped beside the picnic blanket.

'Which first?' she thought. 'There's so much good food. I think that red snapper looks too juicy to be left.'

She crept forward.

Just as she put a paw on the fish's back, there was a loud squawk from above.

"Oh, no, you don't, you naughty cat! You should be ashamed. While those kind otters are helping Timmy, you try to steal their food."

"What? Who, me?" Matilda looked up. "Simon!" she cried. "Simon, you're better! Timmy will be pleased to see you."

"Aren't you pleased, Matilda?" Simon asked as he landed on the grass beside her.

"Oh, yes; of course," she said looking at the crabs. "But you could have come a little later." She flicked her tail crossly.

"Come on," laughed Simon. "Let's go and see Timmy."

Matilda walked back along the tree and leapt up onto Timmy's rail as Simon landed on the bow.

"Simon, Simon," cried Timmy, excitedly. "It's great to see you again. Are you alright?"

"Hello, Timmy. Yes, I'm fine, thanks to that kind old man. But I think our friend Matilda is a little hungry." Simon winked at Frank.

"Come on, you bad cat," Frank laughed. "There's still some of that fish left we bought for you in Victoria."

Matilda stalked off after Frank. "Rotten seagull," she muttered. "No wonder cats chase birds!"

As Simon and Timmy chatted happily, the otters worked away underwater. Captain Jones paced the deck anxiously.

"Got to get going soon. The tide's falling," he said.

They were all so busy, that no one had heard the radio.

Suddenly, there was a long, low 'hoot', like a fog horn.

"Howling herrings!" shouted Timmy. "There's a ferry coming through from Tsawwassen."

Captain Jones ran to the wheelhouse. "We must warn them to slow down. If they make big waves they could loosen our anchor."

The huge ferry came steaming round Mary Anne Point. Timmy could hear Captain Jones talking on the radio. Then he saw the ferry slow down. It steamed past them, hardly causing a ripple. As it disappeared round Helen Point, all the otters came to the surface.

"It's all clear," they called. "We've freed the propeller."

Thank you," called Captain Jones as he started Timmy's engine. "You've been very kind."

"You can finish your picnic, now," called Frank. "We managed to save it for you." He tweaked Matilda's tail as he walked to the foredeck to pull up the anchor.

Soon Timmy was underway again and out into Georgia Strait. Captain Jones put him at full speed ahead for Point Grey. The sun began to set over Vancouver Island, and the evening star appeared in the west.

As they turned around Point Grey into English Bay, the sky above Vancouver suddenly burst into a thousand coloured stars.

"Fireworks!" cried Timmy. "That's the kind of welcome home I like!"

Simon hopped onto the bow. "I'd forgotten all about them," he said. "It's the Vancouver Sea Festival fireworks, tonight."

Captain Jones, seeing all the boats anchored in the bay, stopped Timmy's engine.

"We'll drift awhile, and watch the fun," he said.

The whole crew came out onto the deck, except Matilda. She preferred to watch from the safety of the wheelhouse.

'What a way to end a journey,' thought Timmy. He smiled as another big firework burst in the sky above him.

When all the fireworks had died down, and the boats had returned to their marinas, Captain Jones took Timmy very slowly back into False Creek.

"Well, it's been an exciting two days for you, Timmy," Captain Jones said as he climbed onto the dock, followed by Matilda.

'It certainly has,' thought Timmy. 'And tomorrow Simon will be here to wake me up.'

He fell asleep with a big grin on his face.

THE END